# Bella
## and the
# Balloon

**Written By: Melissa Black**

*AuthorHouse™*
*1663 Liberty Drive*
*Bloomington, IN 47403*
*www.authorhouse.com*
*Phone: 1 (800) 839-8640*

*Published by AuthorHouse 11/16/2018*

*ISBN: 978-1-5462-6794-2 (sc)*
*ISBN: 978-1-5462-6796-6 (hc)*
*ISBN: 978-1-5462-6795-9 (e)*

*Library of Congress Control Number: 2018913315*

*Print information available on the last page.*

*Any people depicted in stock imagery provided by Getty Images are models, and such images are being used for illustrative purposes only. Certain stock imagery © Getty Images.*

*This book is printed on acid-free paper.*

authorHOUSE®

# Dedication

For Natalie.

# From the Author

I wrote this book during my senior year of my undergraduate degree as my honors thesis. I was told to pick a thesis topic that interested me, or that I was inspired to write about. As a pre-business-law student, I was faced with a lot of different choices and options, looking through countless cases and case studies trying to decide what I would spend the next few months of my life writing about and editing to perfection. However, the same concept kept nagging at me.

Growing up, my parents encouraged my siblings and I to find our passions. They took us to countless museums, community events, book readings, etc. and challenged us to try things even if they didn't seem super exciting. We were enrolled in lots of summer camps and signed up for even more after-school activities. They wanted us to find what makes us come alive. The two of them fully believed in Confucius's theory that if you love what you do, then you will never work a day in your life. As it turns out, they were right. For my sister, she was six when she found her passion – and now she is in Medical School about to become a surgeon. For me, I was halfway through high school when I discovered my love for advocacy. I don't know when my brother learned of his passion for working with others, but none the less we all were fortunate enough to find what truly makes us excited to wake up and go to work every morning.

As I am about to graduate, I look around at friends and colleagues who were never given the opportunity that we were as children. So many are settling for jobs that either pay them a high salary or are what someone suggested they might be good at. Either way, it leads to sitting behind a desk and staring at a clock, waiting to go home. There are many causes to this problem, and it is never too late to find one's calling, but I have found life seems to be a lot easier when passions are discovered earlier in life. It doesn't matter if it is science, art, or scuba diving, everyone should know what they adore doing in this world.

That being said, I wanted to take a step to help parents start that conversation with their kids. This children's book introduces and outlines the simple basics of business, but it does much more than that. It shows how to take steps to accomplish seemingly impossible goals. It follows a child who discovers one passion while fulfilling another and learns to seize the moment. My goal with this piece is to start a string of "what if" questions in a child's mind, and hopefully create enquiries that could lead to the discovery of a passion. I was blessed to be put into a home that helped lead me to my future, and my hope is that others will get that opportunity too.

It seemed like it would be a normal day in Cherrywood City. The sun was shining, the birds were chirping, and Bella was in her yard on Maple Lane. She lay with her back in the freshly cut grass, gazing up towards where all the butterflies were dancing in the air. With brightly colored wings and their lighthearted twirling, Bella found herself wishing she were one of them. Oh, what the ability to fly must be like, the chance to float above the buildings and trees without the fear of falling. Knowing that she could go as high as she wanted to, and that the ground would always be waiting for her. She glanced down at her paws and fur, her hopes instantly grounded. Teddy bears don't fly, it was just a simple fact.

"Bella!" A voice called from inside the house. "Bella, where are you?" She turned and flipped onto her stomach just in time to see her mother coming out of the house. "There you are. Remember that I need your help making the honey jars for the neighbors." Bella sighed and rolled back over.

"I will help later, once the butterflies fly away." Smiling to herself, Bella's mom went back inside. Eyes fixed on the delicate creatures, Bell was lost in thought for what seemed like hours. Imagining herself as one of them, and what it must be like to see the world from their eyes.

"Bella! Bella! Bella!" She heard the heavy footsteps of her best friend before she heard her name being called. Opening one eye, Bella could see Ellie rushing out of the house next to hers, clutching a bright green flyer and wobbling slightly. "Did you see this? Did you hear what is coming? Why didn't you tell me about it? Have you gone to see it yet?" By the time Bella sat up, Ellie was hovering over the top of her, talking faster than Bella had ever thought possible.

"Slow down Ellie. What are you talking about?" Plopping herself down next to Bella in the grass, Ellie began waving the flyer around in the air dramatically.

"What am I talking about? Only one of the coolest and most interesting things to ever come to Cherrywood! How have you not heard about it? I thought I was the last one to find out? Oh Bella, it is going to be so amazing." She threw herself back into the grass so see what Bella had been looking at, thrusting the flyer into her hands.

Bella began to read the words on the flyer out loud, "Coming soon to Cherrywood: the county's first annual hot air balloon festival! Come enjoy the amazing colors and shapes of the balloons, and experience what it is like to fly! Bella stopped reading. Could this be true? Could she and Ellie possibly have the opportunity to fly? "Ellie, we have to go to this! We have to ride in one of those hot air balloons!"

Ellie, who was finally starting to calm down, waved her trunk in the air. "I know, but where are we each going to get $25?" Confused, Bella looked down at the flyer. Looking back over the wording, she noticed that at the bottom of the page it said that admittance was $25 per member. Bella, who hadn't even noticed that she had stood up, slunk back down to the grass, leaning her back against a tree. How could just the two of them possibly raise that much money?

Feeling defeated, Bella stood back up and held her paw out to help Ellie stand up. "Come on, we can talk about it as we help my mom. I promised her I would help jar the honey for the neighbors."

As they walked inside, Ellie smiled and rubbed her belly, "Mmmm I love your mom's honey! The best part of summer is when she gives it out. The whole neighborhood waits all year just to get their jar."

Bella smiled, "Yeah, she always makes sure to collect a lot from Mr. and Mrs. Buzz whenever she visits, that way she has enough for everyone." Once inside the kitchen, the two girls and Bella's mom began to work together to make the honey jars. As they worked, Bella and Ellie began to explain what they had just learned about the hot air balloon festival and how they needed a way to earn some money.

**CRASH!** Bella and her mom looked over at Ellie to see where the sound came from, and what they found was the elephant covered in honey, and an empty jar on the ground. "Oh no! I am so sorry, I didn't mean to. It it it slipped away from me, and the jar spilt all over me as it fell." Ellie's ears folded inward as a bright pink began to spread across her cheeks. "I always do stuff like this, I am so clumsy, I'm sorry."

"Darling it is ok, no harm done." Bella's mom began to usher Ellie towards the sink, "these things happen, lets just get you cleaned up." She began to clean off Ellie's clothes, as Ellie began to lick her fingers.

"One thing is for certain; this honey is by far the best snack in all of Cherrywood." Ellie finished licking the stickiness off her fingers and had moved on to licking her arms. As the two tried to clean up the mess, Bella began to form an idea. A plan began to develop in her head so interesting that she had to start writing it down.

"Mom, Ellie, what if instead of giving out the honey this year for free, we sell it?" Laughing, Ellie looked back at her friend.

"Sell the honey this year? Like go door to door and ask people to buy it?"

"Yes! It is perfect. You said it yourself Ellie, everyone loves this honey, they even wait all year for it! So, what if we charge people for it, then use the money to attend the festival?" Ellie's eyes began to light up in understanding.

"Oh, Bella that is a wonderful idea! And then we can have enough money to each be able to fly!" Ellie and Bella both directed their attention to Bella's mom. "Is that alright?"

Smiling, Bella's mom replied "What a marvelous idea girls! But you both need to understand that running a business can be a bit involved, and there are steps you need to take to do this properly. The first step being that you need to call Mr. and Mrs. Buzz, and ask permission to sell their delicious honey."

After calling them, Bella and Ellie found that Mr. and Mrs. Buzz were happy to let them use their honey. So, they went back to the kitchen to ask Bella's mom what the next step should be.

"Well, if you want others to remember where the amazing honey came from, you should label the jars somehow." After hearing this, Bella and Ellie both put their names on all the jars of honey so that everyone would know where they could buy more from.

Then, they loaded all the jars into their red wagon so that they wouldn't have to keep returning to Bella's house after every sale. Bella's mom had mentioned that this would give them more time to sell jars and would be better for business. After, they picked a price that seemed fair for the buyer and covered the cost of all the materials. That way, they would make sure that the two of them would be making money rather than losing it. Lastly, all they had to do was sell the jars they made.

For the rest of the day, Bella and Ellie knocked on every door in the neighborhood, asking if those who lived there wanted to buy Bella and Ellie's Honey - the best tasting honey in the city. They had decided that if they made the honey sound as delicious as it tasted, then more honey would get sold. They were right!

Every house that the girls offered their honey to, bought at least one jar from them. As more of the honey sold, the news began to spread about how good it was. Before long, all the jars were sold, and the girls returned home to count out the money they had collected. With the help of Bella's mom, they counted how much each of the girls had collected and discovered that there was enough money to attend the hot air balloon festival that night. Overjoyed at their accomplishment, the two girls raced towards the festival, giggling about what flying might be like.

When they arrived, there were hundreds of visitors from all over town, laughing and playing different carnival games that were set up around the area. Clowns, cotton candy, and popcorn were everywhere, sending amazing smells and sights all around town. There were roller coasters, and entertainers acting and singing in the middle of an arena. But to Bella, none of that mattered. At the very back of the park, she could see five incredibly colored hot air balloons filling up with air.

"Ellie look over there!" Bella began frantically pointing at the balloons, and the two rushed over to get in line. As the balloons inflated, breathtaking patterns and colors began to fill the sky. Like the butterflies dancing, the balloons began to waltz towards the clouds. It was like nothing Bella had ever seen before. The hard work from the day began to fade away, as all that Bella could focus on was the amazing sight that was beginning to unfold in front of her.

"Bella, it is our turn, we are next in line." Ellie nudged Bella towards the balloon in the middle, one that was covered in oranges and yellows, mimicking the patterns of her favorite type of butterfly. Before she knew it, Bella and Ellie were in the basket of the balloon, floating skyward.

"We did it Ellie! Look at how small everyone on the ground looks! We are flying, just like the butterflies." For that time, both Bella and Ellie were transported to a world of pure magic. It was everything the two had hoped for, and possibly more. When they landed, they overheard the attendant working the station say that one of the spectacular balloons was for sale. For the entire walk back, both the girls could not stop chattering about the experience, and how they would love to go do it all again.

When they returned home they saw Bella's mom hanging up the telephone. "There you two are! I just got off the phone with Mr. Jack who owns the barber shop in town. He just ate one of your jars of honey, and he thought it was the best thing he ever tasted! He was wondering if you girls would like to set up a booth in his store tomorrow, and sell to the customers that come in?"

Bella and Ellie looked at one another, both thinking about the hot air balloon at the festival that was for sale. Smiling Bella replied, "tonight we are going to have to make a lot more jars of honey."

Printed in the United States
By Bookmasters